First published by Parragon in 2012
Parragon
Chartist House
15-17 Trim Street
Bath, BA1 1HA, UK
www.parragon.com

Edited by Samantha Crockford
Designed by James Willmott
Production by Emma Fulleylove

ISBN 978-1-4454-9600-9

Printed in China

Disney FAIRIES

Tinker Bell and the SECRET of the WINGS

Adapted by Lisa Marsoli

Illustrated by the Disney Storybook Artists

Bath • New York • Singapore • Hong Kong • Cologne • Delhi
Melbourne • Amsterdam • Johannesburg • Shenzhen

Tinkers' Nook was bustling with activity. The tinker fairies were making snowflake baskets for the fairies of winter.

A flock of snowy owls soon arrived for the baskets, bringing a shipment order for Fairy Mary with them.

"Goodness," Fairy Mary said. "They need twenty more baskets for tomorrow's pickup!"

Tink watched as the beautiful birds headed off towards the Winter Woods. "There's a whole other world over there," she said to herself.

Later that day, Tink volunteered to help her friend, Fawn, take animals to the Winter Woods to hibernate.

Fawn told Tink that they could only take the animals to the border. They weren't allowed to go into the Winter Woods, because their wings would freeze.

Just then, Fawn got distracted by a sleeping marmot. "No hibernating yet!" she called into the animal's ear. "You do that in winter!"

Even though she knew it could be dangerous, Tink was very curious about the Winter Woods.

While Fawn was distracted, Tinker Bell took her chance and jumped across the border!

Tink gazed in wonder at the beautiful wintry landscape, enchanted by the delicate snowflakes that drifted down all around her.

Then, suddenly, her wings began to sparkle in a burst of colourful light – and she heard the faint sound of a baby's laugh!

The magical moment ended when Fawn pulled
Tinker Bell back into autumn. Fawn touched Tink's
wings and gasped – they were freezing!

Fawn rushed Tink straight to the fairy hospital.
A healing-talent fairy carefully warmed Tink's wings
until they were back to normal again.

Tink decided to find out what had made her wings sparkle. She flew off to the Book Nook, where she discovered a wing-shaped book that she hoped would give her some answers. But a bookworm had chewed through the pages!

A fairy told Tink that the author of the book, the Keeper, might be able to help her. But he lived over in the Winter Woods.

Tinker Bell put on a warm outfit, packed the wing-shaped book in her bag and tip-toed into the tinkers' workshop.

Then, she climbed inside one of the snowflake baskets.

Bobble and Clank spotted Tink and tried to stop her, but her mind was made up. All they could do was watch her go.

In a moment, Tink was soaring through the air.
The young owl that had picked up the basket had no
idea there was a stowaway inside!

As the owl crossed into the Winter Woods, Tinker Bell
felt a cold blast of air. She peeked out of the basket and saw
a winter wonderland spread out in front of her!

Suddenly, the young owl let go of Tink's basket! It crashed onto the landing area with Tink still inside, sending snowflakes scattering everywhere.

Tinker Bell hid behind the basket so that she wouldn't be seen – then she realized that her book had been flung onto the ice. She had to get it back!

Just then, Lord Milori, the Lord of Winter, arrived.
"Now, that is odd," he said, taking the book from
Sled – a winter fairy who had spotted it.

Lord Milori asked Sled to return the book to
the Keeper. Tinker Bell secretly followed Sled.

The Keeper, Dewey, was at the
Hall of Winter. When Tink arrived,
another winter fairy was asking Dewey
why her wings were sparkling....
    Suddenly, Tinker Bell's wings began to
sparkle, too – just like before! Then she felt
herself being drawn towards the fairy, whose
name was Periwinkle.

The girls hoped Dewey could explain what was happening.
He guided them onto a giant snowflake, which lit up.
   "Just put your wings into the light,"
he told them.

The chamber suddenly filled with images showing the journey of a baby's first laugh – a laugh that split in two.

One half travelled to the Pixie Dust Tree on the warm side of Pixie Hollow. Tinker Bell was born there. The other half blew into the Winter Woods and Periwinkle was born. That meant Tink and Peri were sisters!

Suddenly, Lord Milori arrived. Tinker Bell and Periwinkle hid on top of the big snowflake.

Lord Milori was concerned about the book Sled had found.
"What if a warm fairy brought it here?" he asked Dewey.
"If a warm fairy comes here, you *will* send them back...."

Peri and Tink listened sadly. Did this
mean that Tinker Bell would have to go home
already? They had only just met each other!

Dewey told the girls that they could have a little time together before Tink had to go home. Tink put on her coat and earmuffs to keep warm.

When they got to Periwinkle's house, Peri showed Tink some items that she had been collecting.

"You collect Lost Things, too?" asked Tink, amazed.

"I call them Found Things!" Periwinkle replied, smiling.

Next, they went to the Frost Forest, where Peri introduced Tinker Bell to her friends, Gliss and Spike. They went ice-sliding, which was like sledging on a frozen rollercoaster!

That night, sitting outside of Periwinkle's house, Tinker Bell built a fire to keep warm. Periwinkle told Tink that she wished she could visit the warm side of Pixie Hollow.

Just then, Tinker Bell had a thought....

"I made it warmer over here," she said. "Maybe I could make it colder over there!"

Suddenly, the snow floor crumbled beneath them. It was melting from the fire!

Thankfully, a snowy lynx carried them to safety. But Dewey told the girls that now it was *really* time for Tink to go back home.

As Dewey led them to the border, the girls realized
that they might never see each other again. Tinker Bell
quickly thought of a plan.

"Meet me here tomorrow," Tink said to Peri.
"There's something I need you to bring...." She whispered
into her sister's ear.

A little while later, Tinker Bell arrived back on the warm side of Pixie Hollow. She asked Clank and Bobble for help with her idea.

They were hard at work when a few of Tink's other friends stopped by. Clank had told them about Tink's sister, and everyone couldn't wait to hear all about her!

The next day, Tinker Bell arrived back at the border with Bobble and Clank, who were pulling a strange-looking machine. It was a snowmaker!

Periwinkle and her friends gasped in surprise. They had brought a huge block of ice, just as Tink had wanted.

"How does it work?" Peri asked.

A few seconds later, the snowmaker started to grate the block of ice and turn it into snow.

Peri was delighted! The snow would keep her wings cold as she visited the warm side of Pixie Hollow.

Periwinkle was thrilled to visit the warm seasons for the very first time. She saw one amazing sight after the next. She saw a fast-moving rainbow and a field full of blooming flowers. She thought everything was so beautiful!

Soon, Tinker Bell's friends – Fawn, Iridessa, Rosetta, Silvermist and Vidia – all came to meet the frost fairy.

"Everyone ... this is Periwinkle, my sister!" Tinker Bell announced proudly.

Rosetta gave Peri a flower. "It's called a periwinkle," she said.

"Thank you!" Peri exclaimed. "I'll keep it forever."

Peri held up the flower and covered it with frost.

The others gasped as the flower glistened in the sunlight. "It's beautiful!" they cried.

Peri was continuing her tour when Tink suddenly noticed that her sister's wings had started to wilt. The snowmaker was running out of ice, and there wasn't enough snow to keep Peri cold!

Tink took Periwinkle back to the border and, at that moment, Lord Milori appeared. "Lift your wings," he told Peri. "Let the cold surround them." Luckily, Peri's wings were soon healed.

Suddenly, Queen Clarion, the Queen of Pixie Hollow, arrived. She looked at the girls sadly.

"This is why we do not cross the border," Lord Milori told Tinker Bell and Periwinkle. "I'm sorry. You two may never see each other again."

Sadly, the girls went their separate ways. Lord Milori and his owl pushed the snowmaker into the stream as they flew off.

But instead of falling over the waterfall, the snowmaker got caught on a ledge. There it remained, making a snowstorm out of the ice chunks that flowed into it!

Lord Milori carried on, unaware of what had happened.

Later that day, Queen Clarion tried to help Tinker Bell
to understand why the rule about not crossing the border
was so important.

She told the story of two fairies who fell in love –
one was from the warm seasons and one was from the
Winter Woods. One of the fairies crossed the border and
broke a wing – an injury for which there was no cure.

Just as the queen finished her sad tale, Tink noticed
that it was snowing!

Queen Clarion was concerned.
It was very dangerous for snow to fall
in the warm part of Pixie Hollow.

Queen Clarion, Tink and some of
the other fairies arrived at the stream to
find Clank and Bobble trying to free the
snowmaker, which was making a small blizzard.
Everyone rushed to help. Finally, they freed
it, but it was still snowing!

"It's too late," Queen Clarion said quietly.
"The seasons have been thrown out of balance."

If the Pixie Dust Tree froze, there would never be any more pixie dust!

As the warm fairies urgently prepared for the freeze, Tink noticed that the flower that Periwinkle had covered in frost was still blooming.

Tink flew straight to the Winter Woods, but her wings iced over and she fell. She showed the flower to the winter fairies. "Your frost – it kept the flower alive," she said.

Gliss explained that frost was like a little blanket. It tucked warm air inside – keeping out the cold.

"We could frost the Pixie Dust Tree before the freeze hits it!" Peri suggested.

Tink led the frost fairies to the Pixie Dust Tree and they got straight to work. It looked as if the job would be too big for them to complete in time.

But then, Tink spotted Dewey, Lord Milori and the rest of the frost fairies flying towards them! They all worked quickly to cover the tree in frost.

Tink was afraid that help had come too late. The freeze had already swept across the warm seasons of Pixie Hollow and the Pixie Dust Tree.

The fairies huddled anxiously inside the Pixie Dust Tree, waiting for the freeze to pass.

Gradually, sunlight began to stream through the frozen branches of the tree. Ever so slowly, the frost melted. And then the pixie dust began to flow again! The plan had worked!

Tink was thrilled, but then she realized
that she had broken a wing when she had flown
back to the Winter Woods.

"It's getting warmer," Tink said bravely
to Peri. "You should get back to winter."

As the sisters touched their wings together
to say goodbye, there was an explosion of light.
The magic between them healed Tink's
broken wing!

From that day on, warm fairies could cross over the border into winter whenever they liked – a coating of frost kept their wings safe and warm.

Friendships between warm fairies and winter fairies bloomed – just as beautifully as Periwinkle's flower!